Published in 1997 by Modern Publishing,
A Division of Unisystems, Inc.

Characters Copyright © 1997 Tony Hutchings.
Happy Ending Book™ Tony Hutchings.

®-Honey Bear Books is a trademark owned by
Honey Bear Productions, Inc., and is registered
in the U.S. Patent and Trademark Office.

Printed in China.

A HAPPY ENDING BOOK™

The Lucky Glasses

illustrated by Tony Hutchings

MODERN PUBLISHING
A Division of Unisystems, Inc.
New York, New York 10022

Tippu liked sitting at the very back of the class with Monty. One day the teacher said, "Who can name these colors?" "I can!" cried Tippu from the back. "Red! Yellow! Green! Blue!"

The teacher gave him a gold star that day. Tippu ran all the way home to show it to his mother.

The next day, the teacher said, "Pay attention! Who can tell me the numbers on these cards?" Tippu knew how to count to 10.

But when the teacher pointed to number 3, Tippu could not see it clearly. He thought it was number 5! "Move up to the front, Tippu," said the teacher. "You may need glasses."

Tippu told Mommy he hated school!
"Let's go together tomorrow," she said

When they got there, the teacher said,
"I think Tippu may need glasses."

Later, an eye doctor, tested Tippu's eyes. "Yes, you do need glasses," he said.

"I don't want them!" Tippu squeaked.
But there was no choice.
When the glasses arrived
Tippu tried them
on unhappily.
"I'll never wear
them," he said.

Soon, Tippu and Monty went to the Woodland Fair. Tippu wanted to win a coconut, but he just couldn't hit one. He tried the ring toss instead.

At the ring toss, Tippu still didn't have any luck. He wasted nearly all of his rings trying to win a colored top.

"You need glasses, son!" laughed the ring toss man.

"Put them on!" whispered Monty.

"No!" said Tippu. But he did. He took one more toss . . . and he won the colored top!

"You should always wear your glasses. They must be lucky!" said Monty that night. "They helped you win!"

"I guess so," said Tippu, looking up at the stars.

Back at school, the teacher let Tippu share his new spinning top with the class. Later, Tippu went to his old seat in the back, with Monty.

With his glasses on, he could see everything clearly! All day, he answered every question perfectly.

The teacher was very pleased. "Well done, Tippu," she said. "You have earned another gold star."

Now, Tippu likes wearing his glasses.
He knows they are lucky, and he takes
good care of them. Sometimes he
even falls asleep with them on!